Circus Family

by Linda Yoshizawa

illustrated by Greg Hargreaves

MODERN CURRICULUM PRESS

Pearson Learning Group

Dina felt groggy as she pedaled her bike down the street. She'd accepted the early morning baby-sitting job last week. She didn't know then that her sleep would be interrupted by a late night telephone call.

Last night she'd heard her dad murmuring into the phone at three o'clock in the morning! Then she heard her parents talking.

"That was pretty late for them to have been up!" she chuckled to herself as she rode her bike wearily down the street. Dina knew her parents had been young once, but she couldn't imagine they'd ever led exciting lives. Well, her mom and dad could stay up late. They didn't have to baby-sit at eight o'clock on a Saturday morning, she thought.

The light turned red just as Dina hopped off her bike to walk across the street. As she waited for the light to change, she saw something that really woke her up. A caravan of trucks and recreational vehicles was flowing past her. Many of the vehicles had "Fantastic Circus" painted on the side.

The light changed. As Dina crossed the road, she glanced up into the window of a truck. What a jolt she had then! Looking into that window was like looking into a mirror. The girl who looked back was enough like Dina to be her sister. Dina stopped and stared. Then the girl smiled and broke the spell. Dina rushed across the street, hopped on her bike, and made it to her baby-sitting job just in time.

"Thanks for staying with the triplets," said Mrs. Alden as she paid Dina. "Shopping with three two-year-olds can be a three-ring circus."

"It was fun," replied Dina. "Our house is so quiet. There are just the three of us. I don't even have any aunts, uncles, or cousins. It's never dull at your house!"

Dina left. She thought it was funny that Mrs. Alden had mentioned a circus on the same morning she had seen one. At home, it got even weirder.

"I'm glad you're here," Dad grinned. "You're just in time to go to the circus."

"The circus?" Dina said. "But the show doesn't start until later."

"No," said Mom quietly. "The best part of the show is going on right now."

Dina soon learned that Mom was right. The circus bustled with activity. Dina's favorite part was watching the big top go up. Huge elephants pushed the tent poles into place. Meanwhile other people unwound the tent like a fire hose from big spools on trucks. Dina was fascinated. But Dad said it would take about four hours to raise the tent, so the family walked on.

A gray-haired circus worker came toward them.
His wrinkled face broke into a smile. "Arturo and
Bettina!" the man called. He gave Dina's parents a
big hug.

"You old kinker!" Dad shouted, hugging the man
back. "We should have known you'd still be here."

"Does Johnny know you're here?" the man
asked. "You know he was pretty mad when you
blew the show."

"Yes," Dad replied. "He called us last night."

As the man walked away, Dina turned to her parents, mystified. "Who was that?" she asked. "How did he know you? And why didn't he get mad when you called him that name? What was it—*kinker*?"

"A kinker is a circus performer. Years ago, your mom and I were kinkers too. It's time you knew something about your family history," Dad said.

The family walked down a row of trailers. As they walked, Dad told Dina a story she could hardly believe.

"You know your grandparents died in an accident," Dad began, "but I never told you I had a brother. Your Uncle John and I just moped around the house after our parents died. Then we decided life had to go on. We wanted to do something really different. So we sold the house and went to circus school."

"We learned to be trapeze artists and got a job with a circus. That's where your mother and I met. She'd lived in the circus all her life. My brother and I, Mom, and your Aunt Anna started our own trapeze act. We were great! I was the catcher, and your mother soared through the air. But one night I didn't catch your mom."

"That wasn't your fault, Art," Mom said.

"It doesn't matter whose fault it was," Dad replied. "The fall was a disaster. Your mother was in a cast for months, and we were lucky she wasn't hurt worse. That was when we decided the circus wasn't for us. We left. And your Uncle John was furious."

"But why?" Dina asked.

"Because when we blew the show—that's circus talk for 'quit'— John's act was gone too. John said he never wanted to see us again. Until now he never has."

As Dad finished the story, the family reached the last trailer. Dad knocked on the door. Dina had received such a jolt that she wasn't even surprised when the look-alike she had seen that morning opened the door.

"Dina," said Mom, "meet your cousin Gina."

Behind Gina was a man who looked a lot like Dad.

"Hello, Art," the man said, holding out his hand.

Dad reached out and shook his brother's hand.

"Come on, Dina," said Gina. "Let's take a walk. We'll leave the grown-ups alone."

Once outside, Gina looked at her watch.

"It's time for lunch," she said. "Let's head for the pie car."

"I usually have something a little healthier than pie for lunch," Dina said.

Gina burst out laughing. "You must have some strange ideas about circus people," she chuckled, "but then, most people do. Do you think we eat cotton candy and popcorn at every meal? Pie car is circus talk for cafeteria. You can get just about anything you want."

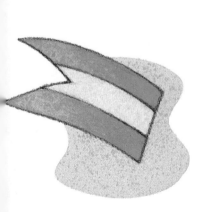

After lunch, Gina took Dina to the circus tent. By now, the two cousins were starting to relax.

"I've known about you all along," said Gina. "Your father thought your mother's fall was a disaster, but it wasn't a real disaster. It would only have been a disaster if she hadn't gotten well. Circus people are used to a few bumps and bruises."

Gina held out her hands.

"Look at these blisters."

"How did you get them?" Dina asked.

"You really don't know much about me, do you?" Gina marveled.

Dina shook her head. "Until today, I'd never even heard of you," she said.

"Well, I've always lived in the circus. By the time I was two, I was playing on a little trapeze near the ground. Mom says I cried if I didn't get to play on it every day. When I was seven, I started practicing on the real trapeze. Now I perform in every show."

"Aren't you afraid you'll fall?" Dina asked.

"Even if I do, I probably won't get hurt," answered Gina casually. "There's always a net below us. And until I got good at it, I wore a safety belt. Come into the big top. I'll show you where I work."

Gina led Dina into the big top. The tent was eerie and felt huge without an audience. A tall ladder led up to the empty trapezes near the top of the tent.

"Would you like to climb up?" Gina asked. "Don't worry. I won't let you fall."

"No, thank you," Dina answered quickly, craning her neck to look upward. "How often do you practice up there?"

"We're on the road for six months. We don't practice much then. After all, we perform at least once a day. But when we're at home, we work on improving our act all the time. And if our act doesn't go as well as we think it should, we come back at night and rehearse."

"Then how do you spend your time all day? Can you ever watch TV? Do you get to skip school?" asked Dina.

"When I'm home I go to a regular school. When we're traveling, I work with a tutor for a few hours every day. I take other classes too. I work out on the trampoline, and I take acting classes. And I learn other acts just for fun. I can juggle, and sometimes I join the clown act.

"And, yes, I do watch TV," Gina added. "We have a satellite dish on our trailer. I do everything you do. I even go to the mall when I have time between shows."

As performance time neared, Gina and Dina walked back to the trailer. They peeked in the window and saw all the grown-ups smiling. The girls looked at each other and sighed with relief.

"Everything seems fine," Gina breathed. "You can come with me while I get ready."

Dina watched as Gina put on her make-up. She put on a beautiful sparkly costume too. Dina thought her cousin looked very grownup. Since the show was about to start, she hurried off to join her parents in their seats.

When Dina found her parents, they both had big smiles. "It's good to have a brother again," Dad said.

"And it's great to have a cousin," Dina grinned. But when her cousin started to perform, Dina couldn't believe she was the same girl. She looked so grown-up and graceful. She swung through the air, let go of the trapeze, turned a somersault, and reached out to the catcher's hands. Over and over she performed frightening stunts. At the end of the performance, she dived straight into the net.

"Mom, did you do that?" Dina whispered.

"Yes, Dina, I did," Mom answered.

Dina was beginning to realize that maybe Mom and Dad weren't so boring after all.

After the performance, Mom, Dad, and Dina went backstage to see the family.

"The circus is the only life for me," Uncle John said, "but now I understand that the accident gave you and Beth a nasty jolt. You were afraid the next fall might be a real disaster. It's okay that you left. It was your choice."

"You have a better act than ever, John," Dad said, "and Beth and I are happy too. We've all done just fine."

"How about you, Gina?" Dina asked. "Will you ever leave the circus?"

"No way," Gina grinned. "I love the big top. The circus is my home, and circus people are my family."

Then, seeing a sad look cross Dina's face, Gina gave her a hug. "Of course, the circus people aren't my only family," she added. "Not anymore!"